Steady, Freddie!

Steady, Freddie!

by SCOTT CORBETT

illustrated by Lawrence Beall Smith

E. P. DUTTON & CO., INC. NEW YORK

Published simultaneously in Canada by Clarke,
Irwin & Company Limited, Toronto and Vancouver

SBN: 0-525-39950-x (Trade)   SBN: 0-525-39951-8 (DLLB)
Library of Congress Catalog Card Number: 78-116881

Designed by Hilda Scott
Printed in the U.S.A.
First Edition

Steady, Freddie!

1.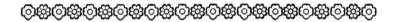

Among the members of Girl Scout Troop 20, Donna Wesley was no worse than average in most activities.

She could build a fire without using too many matches if everything was good and dry and there was no wind. She could identify six or seven kinds of trees most of the time. She could swim a hundred yards without sinking to the bottom, even though it took her about twice as long as it did Patrol Leader Phoebe Jones, who was outstanding at everything.

She could follow a deer trail in the woods if it was pointed out to her by their Troop Leader, Mrs. Burbage, who always saw things like that in the woods. She could sing most of their camp songs without forgetting the words. And she enjoyed most of their activities.

There was only one annual activity she looked forward to with about as much pleasure as an hour in the dentist's chair.

1.

The annual Girl Scout cookie sale.

If there was one thing she hated, it was having to go from door to door and try to sell those cookies. Because Donna was terrible at it. She was a bit shy, anyway, and when she tried to sell anything she became even shyer.

It took her about five minutes to get up nerve enough to knock on a stranger's door. When the door opened, her usual approach was to turn red and mumble, "You don't want to buy some cookies, do you?" To which the natural reply was, "No," and that was the reply she usually received.

As a result, every year she was the one who sold the fewest boxes. Phoebe Jones could be counted on to sell ten boxes for every one that Donna sold, and to win the prize for Most Boxes Sold (she had won it for three years in a row now) while everybody was teasing Donna about selling only ten boxes, six of them to friends and relatives.

The afternoon they visited Standish Park for their Behind-the-Scenes-at-the-Zoo tour, however, the annual sale was still a couple of days away, so Donna was determined to put it out of her mind for the time being and enjoy the tour.

They went to the zoo in two station wagons, one driven by Mrs. Burbage and one by Phoebe Jones's mother. When they piled out of the cars outside the administration building, they found themselves confronted by a group of wild animals that Mrs. Burbage considered particularly dangerous. There were sixteen

2.

of them, and they were a two-legged species known as Boy Scouts. Troop 12, to be exact.

"Major Bliss!" Mrs. Burbage stared at their Scoutmaster with ill-concealed alarm. "Is your troop here to take Dr. Kimball's tour?"

Major Bliss gave her a curt, military nod.

"We're scheduled to go through at fifteen hundred, Mrs. Burbage."

"Oh, well then!" Mrs. Burbage looked relieved. "You're early, aren't you? We're going through at three o'clock."

Now it was Major Bliss who looked alarmed.

"But that's fifteen hundred, the same time as us!"

Major Bliss had been in the army, and always used the military way of telling time, and had his troop use it, too. They were always doing things at oh-eight-hundred or fourteen hundred. Donna knew this because a boy who belonged to the troop lived next door, a boy named Dexter Billis.

"What? The same time? Oh, I always forget how that silly way of counting time works!" groaned Mrs. Burbage, while Major Bliss looked insulted by her choice of words.

"Someone has obviously made a mistake," he declared in a tone of voice that strongly suggested who that someone was. He pulled some papers out of the pocket of his Scoutmaster's jacket with a smug look of assurance. "I have our authorization right here. . . ."

He didn't beat Mrs. Burbage to the draw by very much.

3.

Bristling at his tone, she produced her own papers. "And I have ours right here!"

They were huffily comparing papers when a tall, thin man with an impressively domed bald head and the general air of one of the larger and more solemn herons came out of the building and immediately joined them in looking alarmed. And well he might, too, because he was the zoo's director.

"Dr. Kimball! There seems to be some mistake here," said Major Bliss.

"There certainly does!" said Mrs. Burbage, agreeing with him for once.

There was a three-way summit conference, with much studying of papers—Dr. Kimball produced a few himself—while everybody else waited. The boys stared woodenly at the girls, acting as if none of them knew any of them, and the girls glanced at the boys and giggled and whispered to each other. One or two of the boys groaned and could be heard to mutter things like, "Wouldn't you know it?" and "What a pain in the neck!" Donna saw Dexter Billis and said, "Hi, Dexter," in a low voice and got a forbidding look for her trouble.

The upshot of it all was that there *had* been a mistake on someone's part—just whose was not established to anyone's satisfaction—and since Dr. Kimball's time was limited, they would simply have to display true Scout discipline and take the tour together like ladies and gentlemen.

The boys' troop was prepared for the ordeal by a

4.

short talk from its Scoutmaster, a talk heavily weighted with words of warning.

"I wouldn't care to be the Scout who steps out of line on this occasion," said Major Bliss at one point, and his flashing eyes were enough to suggest a lone figure facing a large firing squad under his personal command. "I expect field discipline to be maintained throughout our tour."

Hearing this, Mrs. Burbage scored by taking an entirely different tack.

"I *know* I can count on my troop to show the kind of training they've had," she declared with a crusty show of confidence that got under Major Bliss's hide in a thoroughly satisfactory way. And with that, the tour began.

The idea of the tour was to show visitors how much hard work and organization it took to run such a fine zoo, one their city could boast of. The Standish Park Zoo concentrated on the animals of our own country, and included representative large mammals, small mammals, birds, and reptiles.

Behind the scenes at the zoo there was more going on than one might think. For a starter they saw the laboratories, where research was carried on, and the "hospital," as Dr. Kimball called it, where sick animals were treated. An opossum named Oscar was there in a special cage, recovering from a stomach ailment. "We hope it's not ulcers, but Oscar does worry a lot," said the director waggishly.

Next they visited the "commissary"—another of Dr.

5.

Kimball's playful terms—where all the food was prepared. There they got an idea of how much hay it took to feed a bunch of buffalo and antelope and elk and deer, and the kind of wet stuff a moose liked. They saw huge sacks of birdseed and quite a bit of fruit for the birds, and lots of meat for the mountain lions and wolves and coyotes and foxes.

All this was interesting, of course, but live food is more dramatic than dead food, and when they went behind the scenes in the reptile house there was live food to be observed. For instance, according to Dr. Kimball, their water moccasin, a very dangerous poisonous snake, was not happy unless he had an occasional frog, so the zoo had to keep a supply of small

green frogs on hand for the water moccasin. The frogs lived in a cage of their own in the back room. Dr. Kimball opened the top of the cage and expertly caught one to show them, and all the girls had a good shudder at the notion of those poor little frogs being fed to the water moccasin *alive,* while all the boys acted very tough about it, and Major Bliss said something grim about Nature's Way.

They crowded around, and since they were a large group there was a good deal of pushing and shoving, and one of the boys pushed against Donna's shoulder bag so hard that it gave her a good dig in the ribs. She wanted to say, "Stop shoving!" but she didn't know the boy, so she just moved away. Normally she would not have had the bag with her anyway, but she had left it at their meeting place last week and today Mrs. Burbage had returned it to her with a little lecture about how Girl Scouts should take care of their possessions.

Noticing the commotion behind them, Major Bliss and Mrs. Burbage both issued some sharp instructions about forming into files and *staying* in files, and the procession became more orderly. It flowed across the big room and around a corner, stopping often as Dr. Kimball paused to answer questions. Donna was well back in the line and couldn't hear everything, or even see Dr. Kimball, but there were others still farther back, so she couldn't complain.

When Major Bliss's attention was elsewhere, there was a good bit of jostling again, but she did her best to ignore the boys behind her, especially when she noticed that two or three she didn't even know were giggling and looking at her, and looking away quickly when she glanced around at them and looked away quickly herself.

The tour would have been better if there had been fewer of them taking it, especially if there had been sixteen fewer Boy Scouts present, but even so it was all right and everyone saw a lot and Dr. Kimball was nice, even if some of his jokes *were* pretty silly.

"It was okay. It was fun," said Donna when she got home and her mother asked how the tour was. They were in the kitchen. Donna sniffed the air. "Something smells good!"

"Dinner will be ready in a few minutes. Go get out of your uniform and then set the table."

Upstairs in her room, Donna slipped the strap off her shoulder and set her bag down on her desk. She remembered the dig in the ribs it had given her, and decided it served her right for having forgotten the bag last week. She didn't carry much in it, and seldom needed what she did carry. If she had known a bunch of Boy Scouts were going to be there to shove her around, she would have left it in the car. She wished girls could have lots of pockets like boys, anyway, and never have to carry bags and purses and pocketbooks. Sometimes a bag like that was a big nuisance.

Donna Wesley didn't know the half of it.

2.

After dinner the Marshalls, some friends who lived nearby, came over for dessert and cards. This was something Donna's parents and the Marshalls often did. First they had dessert, and then they played bridge.

Donna had dessert with them, then said good-night and went to her room. Maggie came along to keep her company for a while. Maggie was a beagle who had been part of the family for as long as Donna could re-member. She was getting old, and set in her ways, and no longer cared much for a good romp, but Donna loved her the way she would have loved an old aunt if she had had one.

At the moment, the only cloud on Donna's horizon was the cookie sale. Otherwise, this was one of her fa-vorite weeks of the year—her second vacation week from school. After the Christmas holidays, in the local school system, every eighth week was a vacation week.

This one, late in April, was the second of these, and the last they would have till summer vacation began.

Maggie settled down comfortably on the small rag rug beside the bed and watched Donna fiddle around, doing nothing in particular, while the spring evening settled down just as comfortably outside and the last afterglow of sunset faded into dusk. Donna dreamed by the window, thinking about the zoo and all the animals there, and wondering if they had eaten their hay and meat and fruit and birdseed and were settling down, too, for a good night's sleep.

Mrs. Burbage would have a lot to say about the tour at their next meeting, of course. She would expect them to remember everything they saw and heard, and be a bunch of animal experts. Mrs. Burbage was all right, but she was pretty hard to live with where the Great Outdoors was concerned. She seemed to know everything that went on out there, and she expected them to learn it all, too.

She was always after them to learn more about "our four-footed friends," not to mention our two-footed friends the birds and our no-footed friends the reptiles —though how most reptiles could be classed as friends was hard to see. Take for instance that water moccasin. He was nobody's friend. He was only too happy to bite anyone who came near; his bite could kill you; and his idea of fun was to gobble down a poor, defenseless frog.

Donna thought about that cage full of little green frogs, and endured another shudder like the shudder

10.

she had shuddered at the zoo. It was all very well for Major Bliss to talk about Nature's Way, but it was still rough on the frog.

Watching twilight deepen outside, Donna tried to picture the zoo right at that moment, when the people had gone home and the animals were alone. Were the animals all fast asleep? Donna chuckled. If you listened to some storybook lady, you might think so, but if you had Mrs. Burbage around you knew better. She could just imagine Mrs. Storybook Lady saying in her gooey voice, "And all the animals were fa-a-ast asleep," and Mrs. Burbage cutting her down with, "Don't be silly!" Because, come to think of it, there was a lot doing in the animal kingdom at night.

Instead of being quiet, the zoo probably sounded like the woods do after dark—like that record Mrs. Burbage had gotten a supply of for the troop. Donna was reminded that she had one of those records at home right now and was supposed to be learning all the animal noises on it.

"Nature's Night Sounds," it was called, and it had everything from a wolf's howl to an owl's hoot. Her father had carried the record player upstairs for her, and the record was beside it on a table.

Somewhere outside a cat battered the night air with a yowl that brought Maggie's head up. Growling under her breath, Maggie got to her feet and left the room. Donna heard her toenails click on the stairs as she went down, and a moment later she was out in the kitchen, barking through the screen.

11.

If a dog and a cat could make that much noise, what must the zoo be like?

Donna put on the record and sat down again by the window to listen. First there were some general night sounds, the way they might sound in the woods. Then there were various animals, one at a time. The animals were identified in order on the jacket. There wasn't any talking on the record, which was one reason Mrs. Burbage liked it.

Donna knew she should put her light on and follow the list as she listened, because she still knew only about one out of three sounds for sure. But she didn't feel like doing that just then. She felt like listening quietly and not worrying too much about which was which. The owls, now, they were easy, except for one who hardly sounded like an owl at all. And that funny little sound a skunk made when you were getting too close for comfort—better know that one!

After a while, along came the frogs, everything from peepers to bullfrogs. They made Donna think of those frogs at the zoo. The poor things probably made some timid little sound you could hardly hear, if they ever dared open their mouths at all. She went to the record player and moved the needle back so as to listen to the frogs again. Peep-peep-peep, chunk-chunk—

"Chur-r-RUNK!"

Donna nearly jumped out the window.

That last sound wasn't from the record. The frogs on the record were still going chunk-chunk—

12.

"Chur-r-RUNK!"

There it was again! And this time she realized where the sound was coming from.

It was coming from the direction of her desk. Her desk, where her shoulder bag was sitting.

She very nearly ran out of the room to call her father, but then she caught herself at the door.

Mrs. Burbage would be disgusted with her. Donna knew that sound, and it was nothing to be afraid of.

But what was it doing, coming from. . . ?

Well, if she wasn't going to call her father, at least she could have some light. She snapped on the wall switch, and felt braver. But even so, even with the lights on, her skin still crawled and her spine tingled as she tiptoed to the desk and reached out to touch the bag, and her fingers trembled as she released the catch on the flap. And when she had flipped the top open, she sprang back nervously.

For a moment nothing happened.

Then two small green legs appeared and got a toehold on the rim of the bag. Slowly a small green head rose between them, and two bright eyes stared up at her.

At once all the alarm went out of Donna. Not only was the animal a small green frog that couldn't have looked more harmless, it was a small green frog with the gentlest, most limpid and melting eyes she had ever seen.

"Freddie!" said Donna.

She said the name without even thinking. It just came out that way.

13.

Why Freddie? Well, Freddie the Frog . . . it seemed right, that was all.

Slowly, carefully, she put out her hand, until she was holding it cupped in front of him.

Freddie looked at the hand, and looked at her, and thought it over. Then he climbed up and balanced precariously on the rim of the bag, with one back leg slipping down inside. He took another look at Donna . . . and then stepped into her hand with the air of a frog who was very glad to get out of a handbag, come what may.

Ordinarily Donna might have flinched. Ordinarily a frog was not something she cared to handle. But this was different, and she made herself stay still. It wasn't bad, either, not bad at all. Freddie felt firm and yet soft, but not slimy or anything like that.

She was surprised he was willing to step into her hand, but then she remembered how Dr. Kimball had caught a frog to show them, and how gently he had held it, and how unconcerned the frog had seemed. Maybe Freddie had been that very frog! Maybe he had been handled lots of times when tours were being shown through, and was used to it. Or maybe he was just so tired after sitting in that handbag for several hours—

"Say, I'll bet you'd like some water!" said Donna, remembering the water and wet leaves and moss in the frogs' cage at the zoo. He did look sort of dried up, too, now that she could inspect him more closely.

Cupping her other hand over him, she hurried into

14.

the bathroom. She ran some cold water into the wash-bowl and gently lowered him into it. When she took her hands away, Freddie stayed put. The way he swelled his sides out and collapsed them again could only have been a sigh of pleasure, frog-style.

Now Donna had time to think about the question that was naturally on her mind.

"Freddie, what on earth were you doing in—?"

She stopped, because she knew the answer. She remembered all the jostling when they were in the back room at the reptile house. She remembered the way the boys behind her were looking at her and grinning at each other, and she knew.

All the grown-ups had been out of sight around the corner. Someone had a perfect chance to grab a frog out of the cage and then put it in her bag while some-one else was jostling her. That was the way pickpock-ets worked, she knew, because she had read all about them in a magazine—and so had those boys, obviously. One jostled, the other picked. And it worked just as well for putting as picking.

"Those smart-alecs! They'll find out!" she thought angrily. "When I tell Mrs. Burbage and she tells Major Bliss—!"

But then another thought struck her, a thought that sent a chill through her. If she did that, if she told Mrs. Burbage—if she told *anybody*—then what would hap-pen to Freddie?

He would have to go back to the zoo, and a water moccasin would eat him.

16.

Gripping the edge of the washbowl with both hands, Donna looked down anxiously into Freddie's gentle eyes and asked a heartfelt question:

"Freddie, what am I going to do with you?"

3.

Certainly she could not leave him sitting around in the washbowl. She had to find someplace to keep him while she was thinking about what to do.

What could she use to keep a frog in? It had to be something that would hold water, and—

Mrs. Feeny's fishbowl!

Mrs. Feeny was an old lady who had lived next door before she sold her house to Dexter Billis's family and moved to an apartment house. Mrs. Feeny was always buying things and then giving them away when she got tired of them. Not long before she moved she bought two tiny tropical fish and a fishbowl and a lot of fish food at a sale in a dime store. When she moved she decided there wouldn't be room for a fishbowl in her new apartment, so she gave the whole outfit to Donna.

Three days later both fish died, before Donna could really get interested in them, but she had kept the fishbowl. It was up on the shelf in her closet right now.

Donna was a great one for keeping things, because you never knew when you might need them again, and this certainly proved her point.

Soon Freddie was installed in Mrs. Feeny's fishbowl, up to his neck in water. So far he had not made any trouble, but she was still afraid that at any minute he might catch his breath and feel refreshed and decide to hop out for a look around. With that in mind she rushed back to her desk and found a piece of cardboard backing from a used-up scratch pad.

Once she had returned to the bathroom and laid the cardboard on top of the fishbowl, she felt safer about picking it up with Freddie in it and carrying the bowl to her desk.

Now where could she hide him? Until she had a chance to decide what to do, she didn't dare tell anybody about him, not even her parents. She could just hear her father. He would be as bad as Mrs. Burbage. "The frog belongs to the zoo, so the only thing you can do is take it back to the zoo. . . ."

The important thing was to pick a place her mother wouldn't notice if she came up to say good-night. Donna shot a nervous glance at her clock and saw her bedtime hour was drawing uncomfortably near. She had better get a move on!

Under the bed would have been fine except for Maggie, who was sure to appear pretty soon. She always ended up sleeping on the rag rug beside Donna's bed. If there was a bowl of water anywhere around, she could be depended on to smell it out and decide

19.

she was thirsty. Donna could all too clearly see Maggie shoving the cardboard aside with her nose and finding herself eyeball to eyeball with a frog. Poor Maggie would have a heart attack—a noisy one.

Donna walked around her room, thinking, and came to the window. She looked at Dexter's house and saw that a light was on in his room.

Dexter! Was he the one who had put Freddie in her bag? . . .

No. Dexter had been ahead of her in line, not behind her. It had to be one of those boys behind her, the ones who were giggling and looking at her, those boys she didn't know. But had they told the other boys about what they had done? Had Dexter heard about it? Maybe. But even if he had, the other boys didn't know who she was, so Dexter wouldn't know she was the one who got the frog.

She felt relieved. Instinctively she felt it would be better if Dexter didn't know, though at the moment she couldn't have said why.

Downstairs her mother came out into the hall. Donna could hear her say something about going upstairs. Her father said something she couldn't catch, and her mother said, "All right, I will." Before Donna could do more than gasp, however, her mother's footsteps went on down the hall toward the kitchen, and she had a moment's respite. Her eyes swept wildly around the room and fell on the cupboard at the end of the bookshelves her father had built for her.

"Freddie! I've got it!"

It didn't take long to clear out the cupboard, not for

someone hurrying the way she was hurrying. There were only a few odds and ends in it such as a jigsaw puzzle, an old pair of field glasses, a bird whistle, a pack of playing cards with two missing, a glass float for fishnets she had found on a beach, a broken folding ruler she was going to fix sometime, an Inca sun-god thing her grandmother had brought her from Peru, an empty cigar box, another cigar box full of checkers and counters, another one half full of jacks (her father smoked cigars), and a box of colored chalk. Everything went helter-skelter into an empty carton she had been saving in her closet, and back into the closet went the carton.

She could hear her mother's footsteps downstairs, coming back from the kitchen.

"Steady, Freddie!" she said, and picked up the fishbowl. Making herself go slowly, she walked it across the room, set it inside the cupboard, and closed the cupboard door.

That is to say, she almost closed it. It wouldn't quite close all the way with the fishbowl inside! Well, it would have to do. Surely her mother wouldn't notice. Rushing to her closet, Donna grabbed her pajamas and raced into the bathroom just as she heard her mother coming up the stairs. Seconds later Mrs. Wesley entered the room.

"Donna?"

"I'm in here, Mom. I'll be right out," said Donna.

"All right, dear," said Mrs. Wesley, and began to busy herself as mothers will in their daughters' rooms, by looking around to see what sort of condition the room was in. "I thought I told you to hang up your uniform."

"I will, Mom, right away."

It took Donna about half a minute to undress and yank on her pajamas. All she could think about was her mother prowling around out there and maybe deciding to look into that cupboard.

Dreading the sight of her peering into it and shrilling, "Donna! What on earth is *this*?" she trembled out of the bathroom and found her mother standing by the record player with the "Nature's Night Sounds" record in her hands.

"Is this that record Mrs. Burbage got for you girls?"

"Yes, that's it, Mom."

"It's quite a record. We could hear it downstairs. Mr. Marshall and your father want to hear some of it again. They loved those frogs! All right if I put it on?"

4 ❀

❁❀❁❀❁❀❁❀❁❀❁❀❁❀❁❀❁❀❁❀❁❀❁

Through lips that felt as if they were frozen in dry ice, Donna heard herself saying, "Sure, Mom." With the helpless feeling of someone observing a major disaster, she watched her mother put the record on the spindle and turn on the player.

"I want to get a handkerchief," said Mrs. Wesley. "I'll be back in a minute."

The instant her mother left the room, Donna darted to the record player. Holding her breath, she picked up the arm and moved the needle, trying to judge where it was the frogs came in. If Freddie cut loose again, she wanted him to do it while her mother was out of the room.

She hit it pretty close. Just an owl hoot or two before the frogs. Still, any second now her mother might return.

"Hurry!" she urged under her breath—and was suddenly in a sweat for fear Freddie *wouldn't* say his piece! Because, after all, he was part of what they had heard downstairs, and if they didn't hear him again they might think it was very strange.

Meanwhile the frogs were beginning.

"Let her rip, Freddie!" she thought, though she didn't dare say it out loud, for fear of taking his mind off the record. Peep-peep-peep, chunk-chunk—

"Chur-r-RUNK!"

The whole cupboard seemed to reverberate. Downstairs the men broke into delighted laughter. Upstairs, Freddie did it again.

"Hey, that's great!" said Mr. Marshall. "Isn't it amazing, the acoustical quality they can get on records these days?"

"Yes, and that one isn't even stereo, at least I don't think it is," said Mr. Wesley. He called up to her. "Donna, isn't that record monaural?"

"Yes, Daddy."

"I thought so. If it were stereo, we'd have that frog right in the *house* with us," he declared, but Donna didn't even hear him, because she was swinging open the cupboard door to say, "Okay, Freddie, that's *enough!*" and swinging it shut again—or almost shut, anyway—as she heard her mother coming down the hall. When Mrs. Wesley appeared, Donna had turned off the record player and was watching the player arm swing back to its rest.

"I played the frogs, Mom."

"I heard them." Mrs. Wesley laughed and kissed her. "They're marvelous." Then she inspected Donna

25.

with a mother's eye. "You know, you look tired. You need a good night's sleep. Hop into bed now, and no reading tonight, all right?"

"All right, Mom."

"Remember, tomorrow afternoon you have to go help box cookies."

"I know," groaned Donna.

"Well, surely you don't mind that part?"

"No, but when they're boxed we have to go out and sell them."

"Oh, now, stop worrying. That isn't until the next day. Anyway, I'll tell you a little secret. Daddy and I don't care if you *never* turn out to be a supersalesman."

"Yes, but all the other girls—"

"I'll tell you another secret. Your father couldn't sell a box of cookies if his life depended on it."

"*You* could."

"Well, maybe, but I'm out of practice. Anyway, what are you worrying about? You told me yourself that Marsha Pritchard is almost as bad at selling cookies as you are."

"Yes, but who wants to be worse than Marsha Pritchard?" wailed Donna, and her mother, in that heartless way mothers sometimes have, only giggled.

"Now, let's not make a mountain out of a molehill, or out of a pile of cookies, either. Stop worrying, and go to sleep."

Mrs. Wesley kissed her good-night and then glanced around the room before turning out the light. She sighed.

"Donna, you're a regular pack rat. I never saw anything like the junk you collect. Have you straightened out that cupboard, as I asked you to?"

"No, but I will, tomorrow morning," said Donna quickly, terribly quickly, with her heart in her throat.

"Well, I hope so. It's practically a fire hazard. I see you can't even close it anymore."

She started toward it.

"Hey, Madge!" It was Daddy's voice, blessed Daddy. "You're holding up the game."

She hesitated, then turned back toward the door.

"Well, anyway, let's do a little housecleaning tomorrow, you and I," she said, and started to leave. She snapped off the light. "Good-night, dear."

"Good-night, Donna!" called her father and the Marshalls.

"Good-night," called Donna, and pretended to settle down in bed. She listened to her mother's quick footsteps go down the stairs, and thought about those words that had struck such terror into her soul . . . "a little housecleaning tomorrow"! Her room turned upside down, every nook and cranny attacked by a determined mother. . . .

"Chur-r-RUNK!"

Donna shot up in bed. Downstairs the men burst into laughter, and then the women did, too. She heard her father walk to the foot of the stairs.

"All right, funny girl, turn off that record and go to sleep," he ordered, but he was still laughing.

"That was great, Donna," called Mr. Marshall. "I think I'll get a copy of that record for myself."

"Okay, it's turned off," Donna called. "Good-night!" And once again everybody called good-night.

Easing out of bed, she turned on her desk lamp and opened the cupboard door.

"Now cut that out!" she whispered fiercely. "Want to get us both in trouble?"

Freddie blinked at her in the light, but made no further reply. Donna hoped her theory was right, that Freddie would only croak when it was dark. However, she couldn't leave the light on all night, and she was willing to bet that if she turned it off again now, Freddie would cut loose again. He was used to being in his cage at the zoo, used to having people around, and probably sounded off anytime he felt like it whenever the lights were off there.

She sat down in her desk chair and stared at him, facing facts. Freddie was not a problem that would wait till morning. Freddie had to get out of the house *tonight*.

There was only one possible hiding place she could think of. She took a look at it out the window. The shed on the end of the garage, the tool shed her mother had turned into a little greenhouse. It would have to do. It might not be a safe place tomorrow if her mother decided to do some gardening, but it would be safe tonight. One thing at a time.

She could manage the trick if she was careful. The house, being a big old-fashioned one, had small back stairs at the end of the hall that led down into the kitchen. The kitchen was far enough from the living

28.

room so that she could sneak out the back door without being heard.

It was no time for faint hearts. Before she could lose her nerve, she went into action. Picking up the fishbowl, she stole down the hall, silent-footed as an Indian—she deserved a Scout badge for Stalking—and made an agonizing, one-step-at-a-time descent of the narrow stairs.

"Just a little more, now, Freddie," she whispered to her traveling companion, who didn't look too happy sloshing around in his bowl.

The kitchen light was off, but the hall lights laid a bright rectangle of gold on the linoleum floor through the open door, and made it easy for her to see her way. Easing the bowl onto the kitchen table, she unlocked the screen door and took the greenhouse key from its cup hook.

Picking up the fishbowl, she inched the screen door open with her back, pivoted through the opening, and held the door open behind her with her bare foot. When it was nearly closed again she let it slide off her big toe. It made the gentlest of bumps, nothing they could have heard in the living room. The worst was over. Seconds later she was in the greenhouse, and the fishbowl was on a narrow table against the garage wall.

Now it was only a question of exactly where to put Freddie. With the keen pleasure that comes from foreseeing correctly a special advantage, she saw she had been right about this being the best place for him. The rays of a street lamp shone through the frosted

panes in the back half of the greenhouse and made it bright inside—bright enough, she hoped, to keep him quiet. She chose a good spot on the second shelf from the top, climbed on a box, and put Freddie up there between two empty flowerpots.

She found a square of coarse screen to take the place of the cardboard on top of the fishbowl, and was feeling very good about her night's work when a clatter of wood against wood shattered her pleasure.

Not that the sound was a strange one. She knew at once what it was, even before she looked around. Maggie had nosed her way out through the screen door. The others had not heard Donna in the kitchen, but Maggie had, and had come out to investigate. And anytime she found the screen door unlocked at night, she liked to sneak outside. That was the main reason it was kept locked.

As Maggie waddled down the back steps and came toward her, Donna glared furiously.

"Go away!" she whispered, and closed the greenhouse door in Maggie's face.

Maggie sniffed at the door a couple of times in a puzzled way, then padded off on her own errand toward some bushes beside the house.

Lights blazed on in the kitchen. With a gasp, Donna ducked down out of sight, and heard her father's voice.

"I *thought* I heard that dog go out! What's this door doing unlocked, anyway? Maggie? Maggie! Oh, there you are. Come in here! . . . Oh. Well, don't be long about it. . . ."

31.

"It was Maggie, eh?" said Mr. Marshall, who had come out to the kitchen, too.

"Yes. I thought this door was locked, but Donna must have gone outside after supper. If I've told her once to always lock this screen door, I've told her a hundred times, but—well, you know how kids are."

They talked about how kids were, and made some admissions Donna was not supposed to hear about how they were the same way when *they* were kids, and then Mr. Wesley called Maggie again. This time she reluctantly obeyed her master's voice and came inside.

The screen door closed. The hook clicked firmly in the eye.

"There!" said Mr. Wesley. "Now let's get back to the game."

The kitchen lights went out like a last ray of hope. Donna straightened up and peered at the house with a tear in her eye and a knot in her stomach. She turned and gave Freddie a look that was downright unfriendly.

"Now look at the mess you've got me into!" she whispered. "What am I supposed to do now?"

5 ✿

Trapped in the greenhouse with a stolen frog in a fish-bowl! Locked out of her own house in her pajamas in the middle of the night when she was supposed to be asleep in her bed!

It was enough to make any girl sniffle, and for a while Donna sniffled.

Then, as the first wave of self-pity subsided, she began to feel bad about having spoken so sharply to Freddie.

"Well, it's not really your fault," she admitted over her shoulder. "You're just the innocent whatchamacall-it in this whole thing. But what am I going to do?"

Somehow she had to get back in the house, and in a hurry. Anytime now her mother might take it into her head to run up and see if she had gotten to sleep.

As she stared at the house, her eyes went to the basement windows.

Inspiration!

She turned around to pass along the good news.

"Freddie! I forgot to lock the basement window again!"

Freddie blinked up at her admiringly.

"It'll work. I know just how!" she said, thinking rapidly now. "If only I can get in . . . yes, it'll work!"

She slipped outside, locked the greenhouse door, and tiptoed across the grass, cool and dewy under her bare feet, to one of the basement windows. It was the one over her father's basement workbench, where she often worked on things with tools he had given her permission to use. When it was hot he always pushed open the window above the workbench. Donna usually opened it, too, though she had to climb up on the bench to reach it.

First you had to raise a small screen that slid up in slots. Then you unlocked the window and pushed it open. It had hinges at the top, and since they were friction hinges the window stayed at whatever angle you pushed it to.

Donna was sure she had forgotten to lock it earlier in the day.

Then a new thought jarred her. Had her father gone down and closed it before supper? She hoped not! Surely he would have had something to say about it if he had. "Donna, if you forget once more to lock that window, I'll have to forbid you to work down there!" or something like that.

She was right! He hadn't locked it. The window was ajar.

34.

Squatting in front of it, she slowly swung it open as far as it would go. Next she got a fingernail hold on the bottom of the screen and worked it part way up. Then she turned, got down on her belly, and began to wriggle backwards through the opening, legs first.

It was tricky, but Donna was determined. Soon her legs were inside, dangling in the air above the workbench as she lay jackknifed over the sill. Just a little bit more, now, and—

Everything happened in an instant. She slipped. Her feet came down with a thump on the workbench top. Her shoulders jammed up against the screen. The screen slipped out of the top of its slots and slid down her back, clattering on the workbench and banging on the cement floor like an explosion.

From upstairs came distant, muffled exclamations, and then a clatter of hurried footsteps heading for the kitchen, where the door to the basement was located.

Without a second's hesitation, a girl with a plan, Donna found the switch that turned on the workbench light. Next she began to pull the window shut. She was no longer hurrying.

More basement lights came on. The door opened. Her father called down the stairs in the gruff, nervous, blustering voice of a man who thought he was confronted with a burglar.

"What's going on down there?"

"It's me, Daddy!"

"Donna!" He came quickly down the steps. "What are you doing down here?"

35.

"I just remembered I forgot to lock the window," she said quite truthfully.

Her father stared at her. Then he put his hands on his hips and laughed helplessly. So did Mr. Marshall, who had appeared behind him with a fireplace poker gripped in his large hand. They both looked much relieved.

"Donna, you really are something!" said her father. "Well, all right, lock it up. But from now on, *please,* remember to lock it up in the daytime, instead of scaring your poor old pappy half to death at night!"

"I will, Daddy."

"For that matter, you left the screen door unlocked, too, and Maggie sneaked out, and I had to come call her in."

"I'm sorry, Daddy."

"Well, I wish you'd start remembering these things."

When she had locked the window he handed her the screen and she slid it back into place. Then he lifted her down.

"All right, now, let's start all over again. Come up and say good-night to everybody again, and then go up and get in that bed and stay there!"

"Yes, Daddy."

She went upstairs with the men, and everybody had a good laugh at her, and then she climbed the stairs to the second floor, saying her thanks fervently and silently. She was about to crawl into bed when something moving outside in the dark caught her eye and drew her to the window.

It was Dexter Billis.

It was Dexter, and he was outside in *his* pajamas, and he was just going up *his* back steps very quietly, as if he didn't want anyone to know *he* had been outside.

What had Dexter been doing, prowling around out there? Where had he been, and why? Did it have anything to do with her? Had he seen anything? Could he possibly know anything? He could easily have been coming from the direction of her yard.

She watched him go inside, then flopped into bed and lay staring at the ceiling, marveling at how much trouble one small green frog could cause a person, especially a person who had not even wanted him in the first place, a person who had been minding her own business and had a mean joke played on her.

She listened for a moment, and heard nothing. At least it seemed as if Freddie was keeping still, and that was something. Tomorrow, when she wasn't so tired, she would figure out something to do about him. In the meantime, she was. . . .

"Sound asleep," her mother reported a few minutes later, after a trip upstairs to check on her.

6 ❀

❀❀❀❀❀❀❀❀❀❀❀❀❀❀❀❀❀❀❀❀❀❀❀

Donna sat straight up, ready to scream. But before she could scream, her eyes flew open in broad daylight, and she knew she had been dreaming. She had not actually been riding on a green frog the size of a pony, pursued by an enormous water moccasin with eyes as big as traffic lights and fangs like elephant tusks.

But then she remembered the events of the past evening, and thought about the kind of day she was faced with, and that giant water moccasin didn't seem so bad anymore.

Freddie was out there in the greenhouse, ready to be discovered at any moment. Mom was down there in the kitchen, ready to discover him. Dexter was next door, ready to make some kind of trouble. She just knew Dexter was up to no good. He was a creepy kind of kid, anyway, full of sly ways and funny looks, with little squinty eyes and a pinched-up mouth. Why not face it? She didn't like him very much. As boys next door went, Dexter was a disappointment. And right now she wished he had never moved next door at all. There was no way of knowing why he had been prowling around outside last night, but the fact that he had been doing so gave her an extremely uneasy feeling.

When she came down for breakfast, her mother greeted her with a long face.

"Donna, I'm afraid your room is going to have to wait until tomorrow for that cleaning. Grandmother Wesley just phoned. She had one of her spells last night, and she's not feeling well. I'll have to go over today and help her out."

Normally, Grandmother Wesley was not Donna's favorite grandmother, but at that moment she almost made it. Grandmother Wesley was a self-centered old lady who demanded a lot of attention . . . but if she *did* have to have one of her "spells," she couldn't have chosen a better time.

Donna did her best to compose her face into a long one to match her mother's, but didn't completely make the grade. Her mother's eyes glinted at her.

"Don't look so pleased, young lady. We'll get to your room tomorrow, if I have my way."

"Tomorrow's the cookie sale," Donna reminded her with a long face that was suddenly genuine.

"Oh, that's right. Well, then, I'll tell you what. Why don't you get busy today and see how much you can do, all by yourself? After all, which would you rather do, clean up your room yourself, or have me get loose in there?"

"I'll do it!"

40.

❀❀❀

When breakfast was over, and her father had left for work, and her mother had left for Grandmother Wesley's, Donna felt almost lighthearted. She had the whole day to decide what to do about Freddie, or at least she had until one-thirty, when Mrs. Burbage and Phoebe Jones's mother would be waiting at Phoebe's house to take everybody to the bakery for cookie boxing.

Leaving Maggie shut up in the house, she went outside and did her best to slip into the greenhouse unobtrusively.

"Good morning, Freddie!"

Freddie stared up at her with limpid eyes that seemed to hold a definite quality of welcome bordering on adoration. He had lost that dried-up appearance, but now there was something else about him, a sort of drawn look at the corners of his mouth, that worried Donna. It took her a moment to place it. Then she knew.

Freddie must be hungry.

The realization made her feel guilty. Here she stood, crammed full of one of her mother's good breakfasts, and there sat Freddie, who hadn't eaten a morsel of anything for at least eighteen hours, to her certain knowledge. He must be starved!

But what did frogs eat? What could she feed him?

Mrs. Burbage would have been proud of her. Because Donna, standing there in the greenhouse in the clear morning light, used her eyes and Observed Nature at Work. She saw a big fly go buzzing past over the top of Freddie's screen, and knew that if a frog could lick its lips, Freddie would have licked his at that instant.

Flies!

If there was one thing she was good at, it was catching flies with her hand. One sideways swipe usually did it. She seldom missed. Four or five flies were foolish enough to be circling around in the greenhouse. Very soon there was one less.

Freddie enjoyed it. Several flies later he was still snapping them up in a way that left no doubt about his appetite. The greenhouse supply was obviously inadequate.

"Don't worry, Freddie, I'll get you more out in the yard," Donna promised, and found a glass jar with a screw-cap lid to collect the rest of his breakfast in. Still keeping an eye on Dexter's house, she was about to slip outside when she noticed a grasshopper sitting in a corner of the greenhouse.

"Hmm." She glanced back at Freddie. "I wonder how you'd feel about grasshoppers?"

It was worth a try. Flies were so small it would take dozens of them to fill up Freddie. She spent a couple of minutes chasing the grasshopper around before she finally managed to capture it, and she didn't particularly relish grabbing the thing, but it was no time to be fussy. Holding it firmly by the hind legs, she poked the grasshopper headfirst through the screen and dropped it in the water.

When Freddie saw it, he really got excited. He made quite a splash pouncing on it. She almost had to look away then, because Freddie proved to be a messy eater, but at least she knew now what to look for, and she wouldn't have to wear herself out catching flies.

"I'll be back," she told him, and propped the square of cardboard against the side of the fishbowl so that nobody could see what was in it if somebody happened to look through the windows . . . somebody like Dexter. When she slipped outside, she also took the precaution of locking the door.

She went behind the garage, where she could not be seen from Dexter's house. There she relaxed a little, and even began to hope that maybe he wasn't home, that maybe he had gone somewhere that morning.

She was down on her hands and knees, stalking a nice fat grasshopper, when her hopes were shattered. Footsteps rustled on the grass behind her, and a skinny shadow fell across her bent back.

"Whatcha doing?"

Dexter's voice was harsh with suspicion. Donna looked up at him with wide eyes she fondly hoped were innocent.

"Oh, hi, Dexter."

"Whatcha doing?" he repeated relentlessly.

Donna was thinking.

"I'm Observing," she decided.

"You're what?"

"I'm working on my Observer badge. I have to observe plants and insects and things," she said, glancing around busily. The grasshopper she had been stalking

43.

sprang into the air and disappeared as Dexter crouched down in front of her and stared at her with his little squinty eyes.

"Frogs eat insects," he said flatly.

Donna gulped.

"So what?"

"You know so what."

Dexter stood up and peered in through the greenhouse windows.

"What's in that bowl with the cardboard in front of it?"

"None of your business!"

"You're not fooling me. I saw you carry something out here last night."

"Peeping Tom!"

"I just happened to be looking out my window!" snapped Dexter, reddening to the tips of his outstanding ears. "And anyway, I had a good reason to be wondering about you, because I heard about that frog Kevin Harris put in some girl's bag, and I knew she must be you!"

"You're crazy! Why did she have to be me?" cried Donna, but she knew she was trapped. It was infuriating to watch Dexter's pinched-up mouth expand slightly into a tight, self-satisfied smile. She sprang to her feet and lashed out at him bitterly. "Maybe you'll grow up to be a detective, you smart-alec!"

But her outburst only seemed to please Dexter. He grinned at her.

"Maybe I will," he said, and from the way he looked

she knew she had touched on a dream. "Maybe I'll just do that. Know what the guys in my troop call me? *That's* what they call me—the Detective! Because I notice things, and figure things out. For instance, I figured it was you because you were carrying a bag on your shoulder, and none of the other girls were carrying one that I could remember."

Donna glared at him helplessly.

"You sure take a good look!" she said, but somewhere behind all her fiercer emotions was an odd sort of pleasure in the realization that a boy had looked at her that carefully. It was all pretty confusing.

"Well, anyway," said Dexter, getting down to business, "what I want to know is, who have you told about the frog?"

"Nobody!"

"Good!"

Dexter was so relieved he flopped down in the grass. Sitting up on his elbows, he stared at her intensely.

"That frog has got to go," he said.

"What!"

Donna was outraged. But Dexter went right on talking.

"He's got to disappear, and you've got to keep quiet about him. Because if you don't, it's zzzzzzt"—and here Dexter drew a finger across his throat—"for Kevin Harris!"

7.

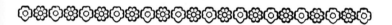

For a moment Donna stared at Dexter. Then she drew a trembling finger across her own throat.

"Zzzzzzzt . . . for Kevin Harris?"

Dexter nodded, and repeated the dread gesture.

"Zzzzzzzzzt!"

Donna considered this grim eventuality.

"But I don't even know Kevin Harris!" she pointed out. "What's more, I don't like him, because that was a dirty trick, putting—"

"Okay, he put a frog in your bag, but he's my Patrol Leader and he's a good guy," said Dexter fiercely, and somehow his squinty little eyes and pinched-up mouth looked less unattractive now that he was talking about a friend. "When I had the mumps he brought me books from the library."

Donna was shaken by this example of friendship. She frowned at Dexter, and bit one of her nails.

"But why is it zzzzzzzt?" she asked.

47.

Dexter gritted his teeth, appalled by such a lack of understanding.

"You don't know Major Bliss! Did you hear him talk to us before that tour?"

"Yes."

"Did you hear what he said?"

"Yes."

"Well, then! What do you think will happen to Kevin if Major Bliss finds out about that frog?"

"Oh!"

Now Donna understood. Now she could see Kevin Harris, a pale figure, standing in front of the entire Boy Scout Troop 12 while Major Bliss stripped him of his Merit badges and all his other insignia and expelled him from the ranks forever. As a Boy Scout, Kevin Harris would be through.

On the other hand, there was Freddie to think about. Why should Freddie have to disappear just because Kevin Harris had been mean enough to grab him out of his cage and put him in a girl's shoulder bag!

But then there was still another way of looking at it. If Kevin *hadn't* grabbed Freddie, then Freddie would have nothing to look forward to in life but being eaten by a water moccasin. It was all terribly mixed up, so mixed up she hardly knew what to think.

Dexter frowned.

"It was a crazy thing for Kevin to do," he said. "He took an awful chance. What if it had been some other girl? What if she'd looked in her bag and screamed when the frog jumped out? Kevin would have been in the soup then and there! It's a good thing it was you! Listen, I'll tell you what. If you'll let me have him, I won't even kill him. I'll take him out to Great Swamp and turn him loose."

"What good would that do?" cried Donna. "He doesn't know his way around a swamp, he's a *tame* frog! He'd just get eaten out there, the same as if—"

"We don't have any water moccasins this far north."

"Well, then, a heron, or something. Herons eat frogs."

"I *know* herons eat frogs," said Dexter, who wasn't a Boy Scout for nothing, "but . . . well, gee whiz, Donna, Kevin Harris is a lot more important than a frog. . . ."

They stared at each other silently.

"I'll think about it," said Donna finally. "I promise I won't tell anybody about Freddie until—well, until I've thought about it."

"Freddie!"

Dexter fell back in the grass whooping in a most offensive way. Donna flushed.

"I had to give him a name, didn't I?" she demanded hotly, but Dexter only continued to roll around and snicker and repeat, "Freddie!" in a shrill, obnoxious tone of voice. After a while he managed to sit up.

"Freddie the Frog! You'd think he was a regular pet, or something."

"If I want him to have a name, that's my business!"

"Okay, okay. Call him anything you want, just so he

49.

disappears," said Dexter, and got to his feet. "Hey, can I look at him?"

"Well. . . ."

"Listen, I won't hurt him, or even touch him."

"Boy Scout's honor?"

"Sure."

"Let's see!"

"Aw, for crying out loud!" grumbled Dexter, but he held up his right hand and reassured her briefly with the three-fingered Scout sign. Donna stood up and took the key from her pocket.

"All right, then," she said, and unlocked the door. Dexter and Freddie stared at each other. Donna appealed to Dexter. "How can you look at him and think about a water moccasin eating him?"

"He looks like any old frog to me."

"Well, he isn't! He's—well, he's not, that's all," said Donna, unable to find the words to express Freddie's special qualities. Then a worry that had been gnawing away in the back of her mind all along came to the fore, now that she had someone to mention it to. "Listen, do you suppose the zoo people have noticed one of their frogs is missing?"

"I was wondering about that, too," Dexter admitted.

"Well? Do you think they might?"

"Maybe. I bet they keep count of how many they have," said Dexter, and now his tone was as anxious as her own. "If they do notice, they'll probably think of us right away—our tour, I mean—and then if they tell Major Bliss, he'll line us up and ask which one of us took it. . . ."

"And Kevin will have to say he did."

"That's right," said Dexter, and looked so unhappy that now Donna found herself trying to comfort him.

"But listen, lots of tours go through, and maybe by the time they count their frogs and notice one is missing they won't know which tour to blame, so maybe they won't do anything about it," she said. And Dexter, ready to clutch at any optimistic straw, brightened up and said she was probably right.

Then he looked at Freddie again.

"Say, I'll bet he needs some exercise. Let's take him out in the yard and let him hop around."

The idea scared Donna, but it was tempting. What was the good of saving Freddie's life if she made him sit in a bowl till he got all stiff in the joints? Besides, it would be fun to see what he did.

"Anybody home at your house?"

"No. How about yours?"

"No, my mother's gone for the day."

"Well, then!"

"Okay, if you promise to help guard him."

Feeling proud of the way she picked Freddie out of the bowl, taking hold of him without any girlish hesitation, and knowing that Dexter was impressed, Donna carried her frog outside and put him down in the grass.

The next few minutes were great fun, because Freddie made the most of his exercise period. He executed several spectacular hops, moved around quite a bit, and finally spotted a grasshopper, which he caught and devoured, much to Dexter's enjoyment. Then a cat appeared, slinking around, and Donna decided it was time to return Freddie to his bowl. She put him back, and Dexter watched her lock up the greenhouse.

"Well, Freddie's okay, but he's still got to go," he said. "He's too dangerous to keep around. Anyway, he did fine just now. He'll take care of himself okay in the swamp, don't you worry."

"Huh! That's easy to say, but—"

"Listen, you get all worked up because dear little Freddie might get eaten by a snake; well, do you know what is one of the favorite things frogs like to eat?"

"What?"

"Baby snakes! So what are you complaining about?"

The thought of Freddie turning the tables on the snakes was shocking, but didn't really change her feelings about him. The trouble was, she was really becoming fond of him.

"Well, I'll think about it," she promised.

"Okay, but hurry up," said Dexter. "The sooner the better, before somebody finds out you've got him."

"I know. But I want to think about it first, and see if maybe I can't think of—of some other way. . . ."

"Think fast, then. I'll be home all day, so let me know the minute you're ready to do something," said Dexter. He stared at her, and once more his eyes were small and squinty. "If you let Kevin get in a mess because of that darn frog, I'll—I'll . . . well, you better not, that's all!"

And with that he wheeled and walked away home, mad again. Donna stuck out her tongue at his stiff back and then ran inside herself.

8 ❁

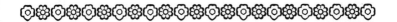

For once Donna almost enjoyed going to work on her room. It took her mind off her troubles. Clothes got hung up, shoes got put in the closet, books went on shelves, notebooks were returned to desk drawers, a map of the United States got folded up, a small candy cane got eaten, and all the stuff in her closet got shoved around in an effort to create order.

She brought out the carton of treasures she had taken from the cupboard to make room for Freddie's fishbowl, and sorted through them before putting them back. During the morning she even went so far as to throw away two or three things, an almost un-heard-of action on her part. It just went to show how unhappy she was.

When her mother telephoned, around ten-thirty, Donna was able to report good progress.

Of course, there were some fairly long periods when she took a break and mooned out the window for a while, trying to picture Freddie alone in a swamp, trying to make herself believe he could live a long and happy life there. But just when she had almost convinced herself, she thought of something she wished she had brought up when she was talking to Dexter. There might not be any water moccasins out in Great Swamp, but there were plenty of brown water snakes, and they ate frogs, too. You didn't have to be a poisonous snake to like frogs. You could be a so-called "harmless" brown water snake and be just as dangerous where Freddie was concerned.

During one of her breaks at the window, Dexter reappeared. He came out of his house and ran over into her yard before she had a chance to duck away from the window and pretend she wasn't there.

"Hey, Donna, let's ride our bikes to Great Swamp this afternoon," he said, looking up at her in his sly manner.

"I can't!"

Dexter glanced this way and that, making sure no one was around, and then glared up at her with a face as mean as a gangster's.

"Stop stalling!"

"I'm not stalling! I have to go put cookies in boxes for the cookie sale from two to four," said Donna, glad to have a legitimate excuse. "That's when our troop is scheduled to work at the bakery. We have to assemble at Phoebe Jones's house at one-thirty to ride over."

Dexter took this news very hard.

"You didn't say anything about that when we were talking—"

"I forgot!"

"I'll bet!"

But then, just as Dexter seemed to be working himself into a fury, he stopped looking so mad. He darted a glance at the greenhouse, and when he turned back to Donna his eyes were squintier than ever. The fire in them had been replaced by a scheming expression.

"Well, if you're sure your mother won't come home and want to do some gardening. . . ."

"She won't!"

"Okay, then. I'll see you tomorrow," said Dexter, and went home as abruptly as he had come.

Boys, even boys who think they're detectives, could be awfully fatheaded sometimes. Dexter might as well have turned on a burglar alarm as far as Donna was concerned. She hadn't missed a thing. She knew what he was thinking as clearly as if he had written out his thoughts on a blackboard.

Dexter was thinking about waiting till she had left and then picking the greenhouse lock and kidnaping Freddie.

The lock was nothing fancy. Someone like Dexter could probably pick it, if he tried hard enough. There was a good enough chance of it to make her feel she couldn't risk going off and leaving Freddie alone in the greenhouse.

But where else could she hide him?

There wasn't another place on their property that was safe, not one other place.

So *now* what was she to do?

❀❀❀

Once again, as she walked over to Phoebe Jones's house, Donna was carrying her shoulder bag.

She wondered how Freddie felt, finding himself back in there. At least this time he would be more comfortable. First she had lined her bag with a small sheet of plastic. Then she had put in some wet leaves. Then Freddie.

The more she thought about it all, though, the more guilty she felt. Not about having Freddie, but about *keeping* Freddie. What kind of life was this for a frog, hiding out in fishbowls and shoulder bags? Dexter was probably right, after all. It would be better to give Freddie his freedom and let him take his chances. Tomorrow—

But tomorrow was the darn old cookie sale, and she'd have to be doing that!

Still, she would only have to go out selling cookies door-to-door, or trying to, in the morning. In the afternoon, she and Dexter could take Freddie out to the swamp.

But in the meantime, she had to protect Freddie from Dexter, because she didn't quite trust Dexter not to do something mean.

For a moment she hated him, but then she felt sorry for him. She knew he wasn't the kind of kid who was popular. He often seemed to be lonely and at loose ends, but he was too proud to play catch with a girl or anything like that, so he hadn't come over much.

56.

She could just imagine what it meant to him when a boy like Kevin Harris did something nice for him like bringing him books from the library when he had the mumps. Kevin Harris, who was a Patrol Leader and probably very popular and good at everything. Donna had seen the same thing happen among girls. One sure way to make a friend for life—whether you wanted that friend or not—was to do something nice for a jerk.

Donna was not late, but even so almost everybody else seemed to be waiting on the side lawn at Phoebe Jones's house when she got there. Mrs. Burbage's station wagon was out in front, and their Troop Leader was having a few words to say as Donna joined the group.

"As you girls know, I'm old-fashioned about a lot of things. If it was up to me, we'd still be baking our own cookies, instead of having a bakery do it. I know that's not supposed to be practical in these modern times, but I still feel it would be more character-building and more in the spirit of what the Girl Scouts are all about.

"I don't mind saying that when Mr. Schultz at the bakery reported his boxing equipment had broken down, I for one welcomed the news. When you Scouts have rallied round and packed those cookies yourselves, you'll be able to feel they're truly Girl Scout cookies to a degree they wouldn't have been otherwise. So let's make our part of the job as good as we can, and show everybody we've got the best troop in town!"

With this splendid pep talk under their belts, the girls scrambled eagerly into the cars. Donna had to do her scrambling carefully, to protect Freddie, but managed to get a seat in the back end of Mrs. Burbage's station wagon next to a window. Evie Roche, who was always late, came running up the street, while everybody yelled for her to hurry, and then they were on their way.

A big square room in the back end of the bakery had been set up for the Girl Scouts' use. The room was full of Scouts at long tables, packing cookies into oblong boxes. They waited outside while the troop that was working finished up, assembled, and filed out. Then Troop 20 took over.

Donna headed straight for a place in a corner, and fortunately when Mrs. Burbage started assigning places she let her stay there. What Donna wanted was to be as inconspicuous as possible, and the corner seemed like the best place for that.

After taking off her shoulder bag and carefully putting it against the wall on the table, Donna turned to listen to instructions. Each table had trays and trays of cookies on it, and big stacks of empty boxes. Each box had three compartments, side by side, and held a dozen cookies. Four cookies were to be placed one on top of the other in each compartment. Then the box was to be sealed with a broad strip of the special gummed tape, Girl Scout green, that was provided in a holder at each place. The tops of the boxes had GIRL SCOUT COOKIES printed on them in green.

The job wasn't exactly a difficult one, but they had to be careful with the cookies, which made the work more interesting than it otherwise would have been. Everybody took pride in seeing how many perfect boxes they could do, without breaking or chipping any cookies, and the time went fast.

Donna was enjoying herself, and had almost relaxed, when she heard Mrs. Burbage and Phoebe Jones's mother talking behind her.

"Oh, that's so! I almost forgot!" she heard Mrs. Burbage say. "What time does the bank close?"

"Not till five o'clock today."

"Oh, then we're all right."

Mrs. Burbage clapped her hands for attention.

"Girls, girls!" She held up one hand, giving them the quiet sign. When they had stopped talking and turned her way, she went on. "As you know, we will sell our cookies for seventy-five cents a box. We need quarters for change when we start out. I want two girls to go with our treasurer to the bank and bring back ten rolls of quarters."

She turned her head Donna's way.

"Donna, I see you have your bag with you. That will be just the thing to carry the rolls of quarters in, so you may be one of the girls. Joan, you've been working hard, so you may be the other."

Someone asked a question, and Mrs. Burbage turned back to answer it, which was just as well. Otherwise she might have noticed that Donna seemed to be in need of First Aid. She had turned so pale anyone

60.

would have thought she was about to faint. An expression of utter panic glazed her eyes. As she leaned giddily on the table and stared at her shoulder bag, she remained in shock for about ten seconds. It was almost like being unconscious.

But then a sort of frozen calm seemed to take over, as though she had become a zombie. She realized that everybody was listening to Mrs. Burbage. Nobody was paying any attention to her. Donna looked down at the cookie box she had been filling, and her hands went out like mechanical appliances and put cookies into the second of the three compartments.

Next she pulled her bag over in front of her. Moving with the same zombie-like deliberation, she opened it, gathered together the corners of the plastic, and lifted the contents of her bag into the third compartment.

It couldn't have been a better fit.

Closing the cover of the box, she pulled off a strip of the gummed tape, sealed it—and then swayed so dizzily she thought she was really a goner this time.

But even now, not one girl was looking her way. Everybody was still looking at Mrs. Burbage, listening to her answer questions. The knowledge kept Donna on her feet. She had gotten away with it!

Dimly she heard a voice speaking to her.

"Okay, Donna, let's go! Bring your bag!"

It was Sheila Fairfax, their troop treasurer, being very bustling and self-important. Sheila had her by the hand, and was dragging her away.

9 ⚘

The trip to the bank was like taking a walk in a night-mare. There was that same feeling of struggling to get somewhere and never getting there. As it happened, the bank was only three blocks from the bakery, but to Donna it was three miles.

When she urged the others to hurry, Sheila only said, "We *are* hurrying!" and Joan told her not to be such an eager beaver.

Why had she let herself be dragged off like this? She could have said she wanted to stay there boxing cookies, she could have offered to let some other girl use her bag. No, she couldn't, that would have sounded funny. But . . . what if somebody fooled around with her boxes before she could get back and rescue Fred-die? There was no reason why anybody should touch those boxes while she was gone, but what if they did?

If the walk to the bank was bad, the wait at the bank was worse. It turned out that nobody had ten rolls of quarters all ready. A teller had to make up some rolls for them, and he took forever doing it. Then he fussed around with the troop's bankbook, checking the files, plodding back and forth. Throughout all this slow torture Donna stood by silently, her stomach full of red-hot needles. She could have killed that slowpoke of a teller. She could have killed her chatterbox companions as they passed the time with bright unconcern. She could have screamed.

By the time the quarters were finally ready and the transaction properly entered in the bankbook, she was numb with despair. Numbly she held open her bag for Sheila to put in the rolls of quarters. Numbly she followed the girls outside and began the walk back, with one girl posted on each side of her as a guard, both girls alert now and nervously on the lookout for possible purse-snatchers.

The only one who was not worried about the money was Donna. At that moment she would have welcomed a hit on the head and a chance to be unconscious for a while. Especially was this so when they turned the corner at the bakery and saw all the other girls getting into the cars.

Evie Roche noticed them and called, "Here they come, Mrs. Burbage!"

Their leader appeared at the bakery door.

"Oh, good. You're just in time, girls." She had the proud look of a woman with a new feather in her cap. "We're all finished up. Troop 20 worked so fast we finished ahead of time! And we're the last troop assigned

63.

to work, so the job is done! Did you get the rolls of quarters all right? Good! I'll take them, Donna."

Another lady who seemed to be connected with the Girl Scouts had also appeared. Preoccupied with talking to her, Mrs. Burbage took the rolls of quarters from Donna without even noticing the white face above the shoulder bag. Not that the face showed anything. Already numb, Donna had not even changed her expression. Catastrophe had lost its power to surprise. She had known all along that something like this would happen to her, and now it had.

The sensation of dragging herself through a dream continued, especially that feeling of utter aloneness that can be so chilling a part of a bad dream. Everybody else was happily chattering away just as Sheila and Joan had chattered at the bank. Nobody paid any attention to Donna as she climbed into Mrs. Burbage's station wagon and huddled miserably in a corner. The other Girl Scout lady rode with Mrs. Burbage in the front seat and continued to occupy her attention.

When they reached the corner nearest Donna's house, she struggled out of the back end of the station wagon, said her automatic good-bys, and began to walk home.

Only then, when she was really alone, did her mind unfreeze and start to function again. It was as painful as when toes and fingers begin to thaw out after frostbite. It hurt so much she began to cry.

The wet shock of tears on her cheeks was horrible. She couldn't walk down the street bawling like a two-year-old! She didn't even have a handkerchief with her, because she hadn't put anything in her bag but Freddie.

She pulled up short and took a huge, tear-stopping breath. She made the best use she could of a short sleeve, darting glances around as she did so to make sure nobody was watching her. And while she was tending to her tears, thoughts that had been dammed up during the ride home began flooding through her mind.

What was she to do? Well . . . one thing she could do was—keep on doing what she was doing that very moment. Go home. Say nothing. Hundreds of Girl Scouts had helped box those cookies. If she simply kept still and let matters take their course, then how would anyone ever be able to figure out that Donna Wesley, out of all those Girl Scouts, had been the one who put that frog in the cookie box? She could simply keep still about it, and then she and Dexter Billis and Kevin Harris would be out of trouble. Donna was only human, and being human she could not fail to think of this attractive possible course of action.

But all the time she was thinking of it, the small, still voice that makes life so difficult was nagging away at her, telling her it wouldn't do. She *couldn't* just walk away and leave Freddie sitting in a box of cookies in the back end of a bakery. What would happen to him? He might suffocate. No, he wouldn't. The boxes weren't that tight. At least, she didn't think they were. But that wasn't the point, anyway. What would hap-

66.

pen if someone bought a box of Girl Scout cookies and opened it up and found a live frog in it? Or a dead one? It was hard to say which would be worse. Either way, nobody would ever trust a box of Girl Scout cookies again. Girl Scout cookie sales would be ruined forever. . . .

Well? . . .

What was so bad about *that*? For a moment she was *really* tempted. But only for a moment. For one thing, even then there would still be this year's sale to suffer through before ruination set in, and for another thing . . . oddly enough, it was not the other girls she thought about when she considered the disgrace that would result for the Girl Scouts. The girls would manage. They would bounce back. Half of them would just think it was funny. No, it was Mrs. Burbage's face she saw, absolutely stricken. It was the grown-ups who were so proud, so concerned, so almost foolish about it all. . . . It meant so much to Mrs. Burbage, and silly as she was sometimes, you didn't want to see her hurt.

Donna was so lost in thought that Dexter Billis ran up and planted himself in front of her before she noticed him. He must have been out in his front yard and seen her coming. Feet spread apart, hands on hips, he might have looked like the neighborhood bully if he hadn't been so skinny.

He was furious.

"What did you do with Freddie?"

She pulled away as he made a grab for her shoulder bag.

"Is he in there?"

"No! He was, but he's not now."

"Oh no? Then where is he?"

It was a pleasure to let Dexter have it right between his squinty eyes.

"He's at the bakery in a box of cookies."

"He's . . . *what*?"

Dexter looked satisfactorily stunned. What she was saying made no sense to him at all, of course.

"I knew you'd steal him if I left him in the greenhouse, so I took him with me."

"You—you took him with you? But what's he doing in a cookie box at the bakery?"

"Well, I had to do *something* with him when Mrs. Burbage told me to go to the bank. She wanted me to go with some other girls because I had a bag with me. So then I had to get rid of him quick."

"You mean, you hid him in a cookie box?"

"Yes."

"With *cookies*?"

"Yes. I put him in one part that didn't have any cookies in it yet and sealed up the box with stickum tape."

"Oh, boy! That's great, that is! That's really great! Okay, you put him in a box—but why did you *leave* him there?"

"Because I had to! When we got back from the bank, everybody was outside, ready to leave. They finished up before we got back. So I didn't get a chance to go inside again."

"You mean to tell me you just got in a car and came home?" Dexter all but jumped up and down. "For crying out loud, why didn't you say you wanted to go somewhere else, or something? You could have made some excuse to get away. Then you could have come back as soon as they left and got Freddie!"

Count on sneaky Dexter to think of an idea like that! thought Donna—and wished she had thought of it herself.

"I'm sure Mrs. Burbage wouldn't have let me go," she said primly, taking refuge in excuses, "and anyway, I didn't have any money to come home on the bus with."

"Don't give me that! You could have borrowed some from somebody!" That darn Dexter had an answer for everything. Fresh out of excuses, with no defense left, Donna did the only thing left to do in such circumstances. She attacked.

"Well, I didn't do it, so stop talking about it!" she stormed. "If it wasn't for you hanging around trying to steal Freddie the minute my back was turned, I wouldn't have taken him with me in the first place, so it's all your fault!"

Dexter clapped a hand to his forehead and rolled his eyes around in a wildly exaggerated way.

"All my fault? All *my* fault?" he said in shrill, rising tones. "Well, I like that!"

"You were just waiting to pick that lock!"

"Now, listen—"

"Don't tell me you weren't!"

Her whirlwind attack was so successful that now Dexter had no way out left but to counterattack.

"Well, never mind that, the point is you *did* take that crazy frog with you and now we're in big trouble! And anyway, I wouldn't have thought about picking any lock if you'd said it was okay to turn him loose in Great Swamp!"

"Well, I was going to, if you'd only waited! I made up my mind on the way to the bakery."

For Dexter, this was the unkindest cut of all.

"You *did*?"

"Yes!"

"Oh, for . . . if that isn't— Why didn't you make up your mind *sooner*?" he demanded, writhing at the thought of how easily the whole mess could have been avoided. He was so worked up he had to walk away a few steps and walk back again.

To give him credit, though, that was all the time he wasted on vain regrets. Dragging a big breath into his narrow chest, he blew it out sharply, like a ballplayer trying to relax at the plate, and began to do some positive thinking.

"Well, we can't just stand here yakking about it," he said. "How do we get to the bakery?"

Donna stared at him.

"What do you mean?"

"Where's the bakery, where's the bakery?" Dexter snapped impatiently, a man of action now. "We've got to go there this minute, before it's too late! Come on, there's a bus!"

10 ❀

He grabbed her hand and nearly yanked her off her feet as he started running toward the corner.

"Wait, Dexter! How do we know—"

"Come on!"

The man of action was not to be denied. They made it to the corner before the bus pulled away and leaped aboard like two grasshoppers. By then Donna was so out of breath she could scarcely speak.

"I *told* you I don't have any money!" she gasped.

Dexter was fumbling in his pocket.

"I have," he panted. "I got my allowance yesterday."

He paid their fares and they dropped, winded, into the seat behind the driver and glowered at each other.

"How do we know this bus goes to the bakery?"

"Well, where is the bakery, anyway? I already asked you three times!"

"How do I know where the bakery is? I only went there in a car!"

"Oh, boy! Do you even know the name of it?"

"Yes-I-know-the-name-of-it! It's Schultz's Bakery."

Dexter stood up and bent over the driver's shoulder.

"Do you go near Schultz's Bakery?"

"Schultz's what?"

"Bakery. Schultz's Bakery."

"Never heard of it. Where's it at?"

Donna could see Dexter gulp. He looked around at her, and back at the driver.

"I don't know."

"Well, if you don't know, Buster, *I* sure don't know."

He called over his shoulder.

"Anybody know Schultz's Bakery?"

A man across the aisle looked up from his newspaper.

"You say, Schultz's?"

"Yeah, Schultz's."

"Sure. They're on Van Dorn Avenue. Lemme see . . . corner of Filbert, I think. . . .

"Okay," said the bus driver, "get off at Dickie Square and take a Number Two. Gimme another dime, I'll give you transfers."

Dexter parted with another dime, received the transfers, and sat down again, looking much relieved.

"I'll pay you back," said Donna.

"The heck with the money," he muttered grimly. "Just find that darn frog, is all I ask!"

One good thing about Dexter, apparently, he wasn't tight with his money, or anyway not in an emergency.

For a moment they both stared straight ahead into space, each wrapped in his own worried thoughts. Then Donna turned to Dexter.

"*Did* you pick that lock?"

"Oh, forget it, will you?"

"Well, did you?"

The vanity of an expert got the better of him.

"Yes."

"I knew it! Was it hard?"

"No, it was easy!"

As worried as she was, the picture of Dexter burgling his way into the greenhouse provided a glimmer of hard amusement.

"I'll bet you were surprised when you didn't find any Freddie!" she said, and Dexter's glum glare made it plain she was right.

🏵🏵🏵

Dexter might be a jerk, but he was a smart jerk, and in that respect he was better to have along at a time like this than some boys Donna could think of who were nice but dumb. Dexter kept thinking of things, and thinking ahead. While they were waiting for a Number Two bus in Dickie Square, he thought of something important.

"What are you going to tell the guys at the bakery?"

"What do you mean?"

"Well, we can't just walk in and say we want to look around. We've got to have some reason."

"Oh, that's right."

"So let's think of one."

While he was working on it, Donna tried to grapple with the problem, too, but before she could even get started it was Dexter who produced an idea.

"I know what," he said.

"What?"

"You can pretend you lost something when you were working there, and want to look for it."

"That's a good idea! Let me see, what did I have with me to lose? Gee, I didn't have anything. . . ."

But Dexter's squinty eyes were looking her over, and he said, "How about your Girl Scout pin?"

"Great!"

"That will give us a chance to spend some time looking all around where you were working. You had your own pile of boxes, huh?"

"Yes."

"I hope they're still in the same place."

"If they are, I can find Freddie in nothing flat."

"Yes, but don't just start grabbing. We'll still have to figure out how to get him out of the box and back in your bag. I mean, bakery guys may be around where they can see us. I'll have to keep them busy while you grab Freddie."

"If we can just have a minute to ourselves! . . ."

"Don't worry, I'll figure that out when we come to it."

Working out a plan made them both feel better. But then Dexter had to get sarcastic. He stared at her hard with a superior expression and said, "Well?"

74.

"Well what?"

"If you're going to say you lost your pin, don't you guess you'd better take it off?"

Donna flushed.

"I would have taken it off before we got there!" she claimed, and pricked her finger trying to undo it quickly. Dexter was really a pain in the neck! He even laughed when she said, "Ow!" and had to stop to suck her finger.

After a few blocks the Number Two bus turned into Van Dorn Avenue. The driver told them where to get off for Schultz's Bakery. One block beyond the bus stop, it was. They walked to the corner and crossed the street, and Donna led the way down Filbert Street to the side entrance.

The door was closed. Her stomach knotted.

"I hope they haven't gone!"

"Aw, they wouldn't be closed up this early! At least, I don't think so. . . . Oh, boy! This is all we need!"

Dexter's voice was reedy with anxiety. He knocked on the door, first timidly, then harder.

They waited, while hopes faded, and all was lost, and—

Footsteps inside! Someone was fumbling at the door. Then it was opened by a man in shirtsleeves holding a push broom.

"Hi, kids," he said, and took in Donna's uniform. "Your gang left already, honey."

Donna swallowed, and trotted out her prepared speech.

"I know, but I had to come back because I think I lost something here when I was working."

"Yeah? What did you lose?"

"My Girl Scout pin."

The man grinned.

"You did, huh? Well, you're in luck, honey." He stuck his hand in his pocket and produced a Girl Scout pin. "I found it when I was sweeping up."

He enjoyed her astounded look, little knowing what caused it. Somehow she managed to force a feeble smile onto her face. Somehow she managed to hold out her hand and say, "Gee, thanks!" That was all she could think of to say.

Fortunately Dexter was able to do better.

"Well—uh—how about your—your . . . I thought you lost something else in there when you dropped your bag. . . ."

"What? Oh! Yes, well, I *did,* but I'm not sure I lost *that* here," said Donna, trying desperately to think of what *that* might have been.

"Huh?" said the man with the broom. "What else did you lose?"

And by then Donna had something.

"It was a charm," she said. "A charm from a brace-let. It was real tiny. It could even have stayed on the table when my bag dumped over. I didn't drop it, my bag just dumped over," she said, improving on that part, "but some things fell out."

Luckily the sweeper was not a nasty, suspicious type of person.

"Well, I didn't find no charm," he said, "but if you want to, you can come in and look around. What did it look like?"

Her legs trembling from the close call, Donna stepped inside, with Dexter on her heels.

"Well, it was a—it was a sun-god thing from Peru," she said, remembering that present her grandmother had brought her, the one she had cleared out of her cupboard to make room for Freddie. Actually it weighed about two pounds, and if she'd put it on a bracelet it would have had her wrist dragging along the ground, but . . . it got her by.

"Yeah? A sun-god thing? Well, look around," said the sweeper. "I'd like to see it."

The sight that greeted them, now that they had gotten all the way inside, nearly made her legs give way entirely.

On a low platform in the center of the room stood several piles of cookie boxes, precisely arranged in neat mounds. The tables around them, including the one where Donna had worked, were bare.

77.

11 ❁

The man with the broom made a general gesture that took in the whole room.

"Okay, where were you when you were here, honey?"

Donna pointed to the corner.

"Over there," she said, and walked in that direction because she couldn't think of anything else to do. Dexter came tottering after her. Together they made a pathetic show of searching for the nonexistent charm, on the table and under it.

"No luck? Tell you what," said their helpful friend, setting his broom aside, "there was another fellow working around back here, stacking the boxes. I'll ask him if he happened to find it."

He left, and they were alone. Donna rushed back to those horrible piles of boxes.

"Freddie!" she called. "Freddie! Where are you?"

No answer. She tried again.

"Freddie!"

No answer.

The third time was supposed to be the charm. It had to be!

"Freddie! Answer me!"

"Joe says he didn't find nothing," said their friend, suddenly reappearing as she was making her third try. He glanced across the room at Dexter. "What's the matter with Freddie? Cat got his tongue?"

Dexter stared blankly, and then understood. The man thought Donna was calling Dexter.

"Oh! Me? No, I was just looking around over here, but— What do you want, Donna?"

"I guess we might as well give up," she said. "I guess it isn't here."

"Well, that's too bad," said the man. "But anyway, you got your pin."

"Yes. Thanks very much," said Donna miserably.

"That's life. Can't win 'em all," he added as they drooped out through the doorway.

He winked at Dexter and grinned.

"That's a mighty good-looking little girl friend you got there, Freddie!" he said, and closed the door on their blazing faces. Neither one of them had a thing to say or even looked at each other all the way to the corner. Donna was quivering with what she told herself was shame and indignation. To have anyone take her for Dexter Billis's girl friend! She had never been so mortified! And yet, at the same time, to be referred to as . . . as mighty. . . . She frowned as hard as she

79.

could frown, but something was singing in her veins.

The sensation was fleeting and far in the background, however, and passed quickly as black despair descended on her. Her despair got lots of help from Dexter's opening remark when he finally found his voice again.

"Well, we've had it," he said. "Now we've really had it. If Freddie's in the middle of one of those piles, he's suffocated by now. He's dead."

Tears started into Donna's eyes. The horror of it! What had Freddie done to deserve such a fate? And it was all her fault. Well, and Dexter's. Dexter, that jerk! . . . No, that wasn't fair. Not altogether, anyway. Dexter had certainly tried. He had done his best.

"Well, maybe he's not in the middle. Maybe he's where he can still get enough air in his box," said Donna, not because she really believed it, but because she could not face the thought of Freddie slowly choking to death, buried alive in a mound of Girl Scout cookies.

"Well, I hope you're right," said Dexter, "but I'll bet you aren't."

They walked across the street and down to the nearest bus stop in silence. Then Dexter gave off a gloomy snort, like someone having a laugh at his own funeral.

"Freddie!" he said. "How did you like that guy calling me Freddie!"

"Well, you were pretty smart, the way you caught on," said Donna, giving the devil his due. But now Dexter was beyond the consolations of vanity. He only shrugged.

It was strange, how a person made a person feel. If Dexter had perked up and got that conceited look on his face, she would have wished she hadn't said anything at all. But when he didn't, she felt the urge to compliment him some more.

"You sure thought fast when he handed me that pin, too."

"Well, you were okay yourself, coming up with that sun-god thing. Wasn't it just our luck that some dumb Girl Scout really lost a pin there?"

"I nearly fell over when he pulled it out."

"So did I."

Then they were silent again, each withdrawing into private thoughts. They waited for the Number Two. It came. They got on. It lumbered back to Dickie Square. They changed and headed for home on a crowded bus.

After a while some seats opened up and they sat down. As they did, a rattle from Donna's bag reminded her that now she had two Girl Scout pins. It also reminded her she was "out of uniform," as Mrs. Burbage might have called it and military Major Bliss certainly would have. She opened her bag and took out the two pins.

"Now I don't even know which one is mine. Oh, well. . . ." She selected one and pinned it in place. "Now I've got to turn in the other one to Mrs. Burbage, so she can send it to Headquarters and find out who lost it."

Dexter gave her a stupefied look.

"Are you crazy?"

"What do you mean?"

"You can't give that to her! How would you explain it? Listen, don't you understand? I've been thinking this whole thing through, and there's only one thing left to do now."

"What?"

"Clam up."

"What do you mean?"

He meant exactly what she thought he meant.

"I mean, keep still. Look, we did everything we could, but Freddie's had it. So now, we keep still. How's anyone ever going to know you're the one that put a frog in that box? Nobody will ever know but you and me."

"And Kevin Harris, and all the boys who knew he took Freddie and put him in my bag. They'll all guess when they hear about it."

"Well, *they'll* never say anything, I'll guarantee you that! And anyway, who says they'll ever hear about it? Who says anyone will? Maybe whoever gets the box with Freddie in it won't bother to report it."

"Ha! If you got a box of cookies with a dead frog in it, wouldn't you complain about it?"

Dexter's squinty eyes grew shifty, but he persisted.

"Maybe not. Maybe not. Listen, people only buy those cookies to help out the Girl Scouts—"

"Yes, but they still want cookies for their money, and not dead frogs!"

"Okay, okay!" Hard-pressed, he still sought doggedly for fresh arguments. "Listen, maybe that box won't get sold. Maybe whoever buys it won't really like cookies. Maybe they won't get around to opening it right away —maybe they'll *never* open it. . . ."

But Dexter's arguments were thinning out. If you held them up to the light, you could see through them. His voice trailed off and he gave up, aware that his wishful thinking was becoming so flimsy he could not even believe in it himself. Listening to him, Donna had felt her scorn growing for both of them— for Dexter's weasel words, and for the way she was letting herself even listen.

There *was* only one way out, and now she saw what it was. They had tried tricks, and lies, and evasions—a lie, her mother said, was the intention to deceive—and none of it had worked.

Knowing how Dexter would react was a great help in giving her the will power to stand up and pull the cord that signaled the bus driver to stop at the next stop. Taken by surprise, Dexter twisted around for a look out the window.

"Hey, what are you doing? This isn't our stop!"

"I'm not going home. I'm going to Mrs. Burbage's house. And don't worry about your dear little Kevin Harris," she added in a biting tone, before Dexter could protest. "I'm going to tell her *I* took Freddie."

When there was already so much blame she would have to take anyway, a little more hardly seemed to matter.

For Dexter, of course, her decision was a bolt from the blue. He actually turned pale.

"You can't do that!"

She gave him a final, contemptuous glance.

"Oh, don't worry, you're safe!" she said, and flounced away, high and mighty now, as the bus swung in to the curb.

She did not want to look back, but when she reached the sidewalk and the bus doors had closed behind her, she could not resist glancing up at Dexter.

He was watching her, but turned away quickly when their eyes met. His face looked as if she had slapped it.

Then the bus rolled away, and she was standing at the bus stop, alone.

12 ❀

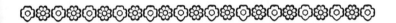

Mrs. Burbage's house was not far from the bus stop. When Donna got there, the station wagon was in the driveway.

Her mind was made up, but her heart was not sure it wanted any part of this business, judging from the painful, protesting way it was pounding. No doorbell, not even those she faced during cookie sales, had ever been harder to press. And the sound that resulted seemed as startling and as strident as one of those alarm bells set off by a prison break in a movie.

The door opened. Mrs. Burbage looked out at her, and this time she saw how white Donna's face was.

"Why, Donna! What's the matter, dear?"

The only way to tell what she had to tell was to blurt it out at once.

"There's a frog in one of our cookie boxes!"

Her leader blinked.

"Er—how's that again, dear?"

85.

"There's a frog in a cookie box at the bakery!"

In any other circumstances the look her announcement brought to Mrs. Burbage's face would have been good for a laugh. The poor woman stared at Donna as though fearful that one of them had lost her mind and she wasn't sure which one.

"Donna, come in here!"

She followed Mrs. Burbage into the living room. The other Girl Scout lady was sitting there, the one who had been with them in the car coming home.

"Now, then, Donna. What do you mean, there's a frog in one of our cookie boxes?"

When Donna looked at her, the other lady smiled and stood up.

"If you'd like to talk to Mrs. Burbage in private—"

"This is Mrs. Larch, Donna, she's in charge of our Girl Scout publicity."

Publicity! That was almost funny, too. But Donna decided she did not want her to go. Mrs. Larch looked nice, and it was easier to have someone else there and not have to face Mrs. Burbage alone.

"I don't care, Mrs. Larch. You can stay if you want to."

"Well, naturally I'm all ears," admitted Mrs. Larch. "What's all this about a frog in a cookie box?"

"Yes," said Mrs. Burbage, "how do you know there's one in one?"

"Because," said Donna, "I put him there."

"Don-na!" Her name came out in a two-tone banshee wail. "A frog?"

"Yes."

"A live frog?"

"Yes," said Donna, hoping it was so.

Nothing in the Girl Scout *Handbook* had prepared Mrs. Burbage for an emergency such as this. Wild-eyed, she struggled for words.

"But, Donna, why would you . . . why would any-one . . . where did you get a frog to *put* in?"

"From the zoo. When we were there, I—I took him."

The words stuck in her throat, but she got them out. Another lie. Did this one count as a white lie? She could only hope so.

"You took him? Donna, why on earth did you take a frog?"

She gulped.

"I didn't want him to be eaten by a water moccasin," she said, and was conscious that Mrs. Larch's lips twitched into a smile that went as quickly as it came. In the meantime, Mrs. Burbage was collapsing into a chair.

"I had him in my bag today because I was trying to make up my mind what to do with him," Donna went on, eager now to get the whole story off her chest. "Then you told me to go to the bank with Sheila be-cause I had my bag to carry the money in, and I had to do something with Freddie."

Mrs. Burbage cocked her head as though not sure she had heard correctly.

"Freddie?"

87.

Feeling foolish, Donna said, "Well, that's what I call him."

"Freddie the Frog," said Mrs. Larch, and Donna nodded.

"So then I put Freddie in a cookie box and stuck that stickum stuff on it, and when we got back everyone was leaving and I never had a chance to put him in my bag again."

During the discussion that followed, Donna was glad Mrs. Larch was there. Mrs. Burbage would probably have become hysterical without her friend's steadying influence. Every time the leader's voice grew shrill and wisps of hair started falling in front of her eyes, Mrs. Larch calmed her down.

"Now, don't panic, Norma," she said. "We'll work this out somehow."

"But, Peggy, what are we going to do?" cried Mrs. Burbage. "We can't go down there and open up thousands of cookie boxes, hunting for a frog!"

A crease appeared between Mrs. Larch's cool blue eyes. She was younger than Mrs. Burbage, probably about the same age as Donna's mother. Her face was thin and shrewd, and there was an air of sharp but not unkind humor about her.

"Maybe Freddie will make a wet spot on his box," she suggested.

"I had a piece of plastic lying under him," Donna was sorry to say.

"Hmm. Well. . . . If we weighed each box. . . ."

Mrs. Burbage shook her head helplessly.

"One of those little green frogs would weigh about the same as four cookies."

Donna did not find it easy to look the others in the face. Every time her eyes met Mrs. Burbage's, she got that how-could-you look. And confronted with Mrs. Larch's cool intelligence, she felt stupid. So she looked away, letting her eyes stray around the room, staring absently at the furniture, the books on the shelves, the television set, the record player with the stack of records beside it. . . .

The room seemed to light up.

"I know!" she cried.

But was Freddie still alive? Well, he just had to be, that was all. Until she knew differently, she had to believe the best instead of the worst.

"I know how we can find him!" she said.

Startled by Donna, the two women stared at her.

"How?"

"If we play that 'Nature's Night Sounds' record, he'll make a noise!"

As Donna explained what she meant, even Mrs. Burbage began to look hopeful. Mrs. Larch stood up.

"And you think if we went to the bakery and played the record for him, he'd sound off again?"

"Yes!"

"Norma, do you have a copy of the record?"

"Yes!"

"And that's a portable record player, isn't it?"

"Yes!"

"Then let's get a move on, before the bakery closes!"

❁❁❁

Mr. Burbage came home just as they were leaving, in time for his wife to tell him where they were going.

"I can't explain now, I'll tell you all about it later, and if I'm not home by suppertime there's a meat loaf in the oven!" she said breathlessly. They left him standing on the front porch, scratching his head.

Mrs. Larch went in the front way at the bakery and got someone to let them in through the side door on Filbert Street.

"We just made it," she reported in a low voice, once they were alone in the back room. "They were ready to close for the day. I told Mr. Schultz we wanted to do some arranging. He said we could stay as long as we like and let ourselves out. So now we'd better wait a few minutes till everyone's left before we do anything."

When Mrs. Burbage saw the stacks of cookie boxes, she moaned.

"Oh, they've piled them all together!"

To Donna the stacks looked as grim as gravestones. Was one of them poor Freddie's tomb? The same question seemed to be troubling Mrs. Larch.

"Good grief! If that frog's in the center of one of those piles, he's a goner. He might as well be sealed up in a. . . . Well, we'll just have to hope he's in one of the boxes on top."

"I was at that table over in the corner. Maybe they took my boxes last," said Donna, trying hard not to give up.

90.

"Well, come on, let's get this record player set up."
Mrs. Larch put it on a table. "Donna, see if the cord
will reach to that outlet."

Donna stretched out the cord, and found it would.

Someone called from the other room.

"Okay, Mrs. Larch, it's all yours."

She hurried to an inside door.

"Thank you, Mr. Schultz! We'll make sure the door
is locked when we leave. Good-night."

"Good-night."

They could hear a shuffle of footsteps, and snatches
of conversation, and a door slam. Silence, sudden and
startling, seemed to tingle in the air. Then Mrs. Larch
turned back from the door.

"All right. Put on the record."

Now Mrs. Burbage took over.

First she held up her hand to give them the quiet
sign. They both nodded. She was right, of course.
From now on, the quieter they were, the more likely
Freddie would be to respond to the record, even
though he had lived at the zoo and was used to people.

She gave the player knob a twist. The record
dropped. The arm swung out and down.

Slowly, gradually, sounds of the woods at night filled
the room. Donna pressed her hands against her cheeks
and waited. The suspense was terrible. What if it
didn't work? What if Freddie was too scared to answer?
What if . . . he couldn't?

The individual animal noises had begun. Soon the
frogs would start croaking. Donna's hands were press-
ing so hard by now they made her jaws ache, but she

had to do something to make herself wait it out.

Here came the frogs! Peep-peep-peep, chunk-chunk. Nothing.

She felt more than saw the two disappointed women glance at her, and she knew tears were running down her cheeks, but she didn't care. At another time the stacks of cookie boxes might not have seemed so formidable, but right now they looked like a mountain range. Mrs. Burbage had said it would ruin everything if they had to slit all the tapes on all the boxes. Anyone would be able to see they had been tampered with. So the worst that could happen had happened. And yet, that was not why she was crying. She was crying because Freddie was in there somewhere, dead, and she felt as if she had killed him with her own hands.

Dully she was conscious of the record still playing, of the frogs making their sounds again. Peep-peep-peep, chunk-chunk—

"Chur-r-runk. . . ."

13 ❀

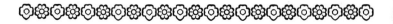

Was it her imagination? Had she really heard something? She turned to the others, and saw good news in their faces. They had heard it, too.

"That's him!"

"Oh, where did it come from?"

"Start the record again!" said Mrs. Burbage. "Here, I'll do it myself. I'll just move the needle back a little way. . . ."

"Let's each stand near a pile and listen hard," said Mrs. Larch.

Mrs. Burbage moved the needle back. Peep-peep-peep, chunk-chunk—

"Chur-r-runk. . . ."

The sound was muffled and small. To Donna it sounded like a feeble call for help. Tensely she moved in the direction she thought it had come from. Peep-peep-peep, chunk-chunk—

"Chur-r-runk!"

94.

This time one of the top boxes seemed to vibrate. Donna pointed to it.

"I'm sure this is the one! I saw it move!"

"Open it!"

Donna picked up the box and clawed at the tape with a fingernail—fortunately she had one left she hadn't bitten off. The tape split. She swung the box top open.

A small green face appeared.

"Freddie! Oh, you're all right!"

The soft brown eyes seemed infinitely glad to see her. With trembling hands, being very careful, she carried the box to a table.

Mrs. Burbage looked like a woman whose doctor had just told her she was going to live after all. Mrs. Larch inspected Freddie over Donna's shoulder, and her chuckle was shaky with relief.

"Well!" she said. "Freddie, I think you were born lucky!"

"I can't believe my eyes!" gasped Mrs. Burbage. And now that the day was saved, now that disaster no longer threatened, there was time for some proper indignation.

She turned on Donna. "Donna, how could you *do* such a thing? Do you realize what—"

But then all of them except Freddie leaped about a foot in the air. Because suddenly someone was banging on the side door.

"Hello? Mrs. Burbage? Are you there?"

The voice was familiar to at least two of them. Mrs. Larch turned wide eyes toward Mrs. Burbage.

"Who's that?" she hissed in a whisper.

Mrs. Burbage seemed to be shuddering.

"That's Major Bliss."

The crisp, military tone was unmistakable.

"Oh, no!" Apparently Mrs. Larch had heard of him. Mrs. Burbage glared at the door.

"What is *that* busybody doing here, I'd like to know!"

"I can't imagine, but we'd better find out. We can't just stand here whispering," said Mrs. Larch as the Scoutmaster hammered again and cried, "Mrs. Burbage! It's Major Bliss!"

Mrs. Burbage sighed sharply.

"Yes, Major!" she said, and went to the door.

Donna was not a computer, and not being one she had received information faster than she could handle it. When she suddenly heard that Major Bliss, of all people, was outside, she simply switched off her set, so to speak. She ceased for the moment to receive signals. It never occurred to her that when Mrs. Burbage opened the door and permitted the Scoutmaster to enter, he would be followed by Dexter Billis and another boy wearing an extremely sheepish expression on his otherwise acceptable face.

Major Bliss's face was long. It was grim. It was anxious. It was not, however, the face of a man who had been let down.

Even in ordinary clothes, without a uniform, he retained his parade-ground voice and manner. His first question, barked breathlessly, nearly floored Mrs. Burbage.

"Did you find the frog?"

She managed a faint, "Yes."

"Ah! Thank heaven for that!" cried the Scoutmaster, and his change of expression resembled that of those people in TV commercials who find instant relief from pain. He swept a hand in the direction of his two Scouts, and his ruddy face was glowing now, glowing with pride. "Billis and Harris here came straight to me with the whole story. They weren't about to hide behind a girl's skirts. Then your husband told us where you were, and we hurried here."

His remarks only added to Mrs. Burbage's confusion, of course. It was Mrs. Larch who came up with a simple question.

"Major Bliss, what are you talking about?"

"Eh? Oh! Of course, of course. Naturally, you don't know. I gather this young lady shouldered the blame," he said, indicating Donna. "Well, the truth is that Harris here put the frog in her bag. Right, Harris?"

Kevin Harris lifted a red face briefly.

"Yes, sir."

"And when this young lady told Billis what she intended to do, he immediately telephoned Harris and they got together and decided to come to me and make a full confession. Right, Billis?"

The second red face responded.

"Yes, sir."

Dexter's hangdog air and mumbled reply were not the usual marks of a hero; in fact, no one had ever looked less heroic—except to Donna. Squinty-eyed, tight-lipped, sneaky Dexter Billis had gone to *his* hero and talked him into facing Major Bliss! Something important had happened to Dexter, and she knew he would never be quite the same little jerk again, not to her, not to anybody.

"Well, I think this matter is cleared up now to everybody's satisfaction," said the Scoutmaster some minutes later as he wiped the tears from his eyes. They were not unmanly tears. They were the tears of a man who had laughed harder than Donna had ever dreamed he might laugh at anything.

When Mrs. Larch had urged Donna to tell her story, and when Donna had described some of the awful troubles she had had, sneaking outside and back into the house and all that, Major Bliss had slapped his knee as if it were the funniest thing he'd ever heard. The women had laughed, too, and even the boys had grinned nervously, but it was the Major who really had a good time for himself.

Looking around at them all now, he coughed a small, discreet cough as he added, "Of course, I see nothing to be gained by spreading this story about. Neither your cookie sale nor Scout morale would stand to benefit."

"I couldn't agree with you more!" said Mrs. Burbage.

Mrs. Larch sighed.

"As a former newspaperwoman, it kills me to pass up such a good story," she said, "but I'm afraid you're right, Major."

"Good. These two Scouts will be quietly disciplined, and that will end the matter."

Then Mrs. Larch brought up the question Donna had been afraid to ask.

"And what about Freddie?"

"Freddie? Oh, yes—the frog. Well, he's definitely our responsibility. I'll take it on myself to square things with Dr. Kimball at the zoo," said Major Bliss, and Donna's heart sank with a sickening plunge. She

remembered all too well his grim comments on Nature's Way. "One of Billis's and Harris's extra activities will be to go out to Great Swamp and collect at least a dozen frogs for Dr. Kimball."

He turned and carefully picked up the box with Freddie in it.

"As for this particular frog, however, I think even Dr. Kimball will readily agree there's only one possible thing we can do with it."

Why did Dexter and Kevin and the others in their troop put up with this ridiculous man, with his strutting mannerisms and his silly military ways? Donna found out as his eyes, suddenly keen and understanding, looked down straight into her heart.

He held out the box to her, and she took it, and right in front of all those people Freddie sat up on his front legs and went, "Chur-r-RUNK!"

ABOUT THE AUTHOR: Scott Corbett has contributed many titles to the shelves of children's books. Among them are *The Cave Above Delphi, Pippa Passes,* and *Ever Ride a Dinosaur?* Mr. Corbett, a graduate of the University of Missouri School of Journalism, lives in Providence, Rhode Island, when he and his wife are not embarked on their far-flung travels.

ABOUT THE ARTIST: Lawrence Beall Smith is equally noted for his book illustrations and his paintings. Some of the children's books he has illustrated are *A Boy and His Room* and *Girls Are Silly* by Ogden Nash and *Toby and the Nighttime* by Paul Horgan. The shaded line drawings for *Steady, Freddie!* capture the humorous quality of the text. Mr. Smith and his artist-wife live in Cross River, New York.

ABOUT THE BOOK: The text display type is set in Corvinus Light and the text type is set in Baskerville. The book is printed by offset.